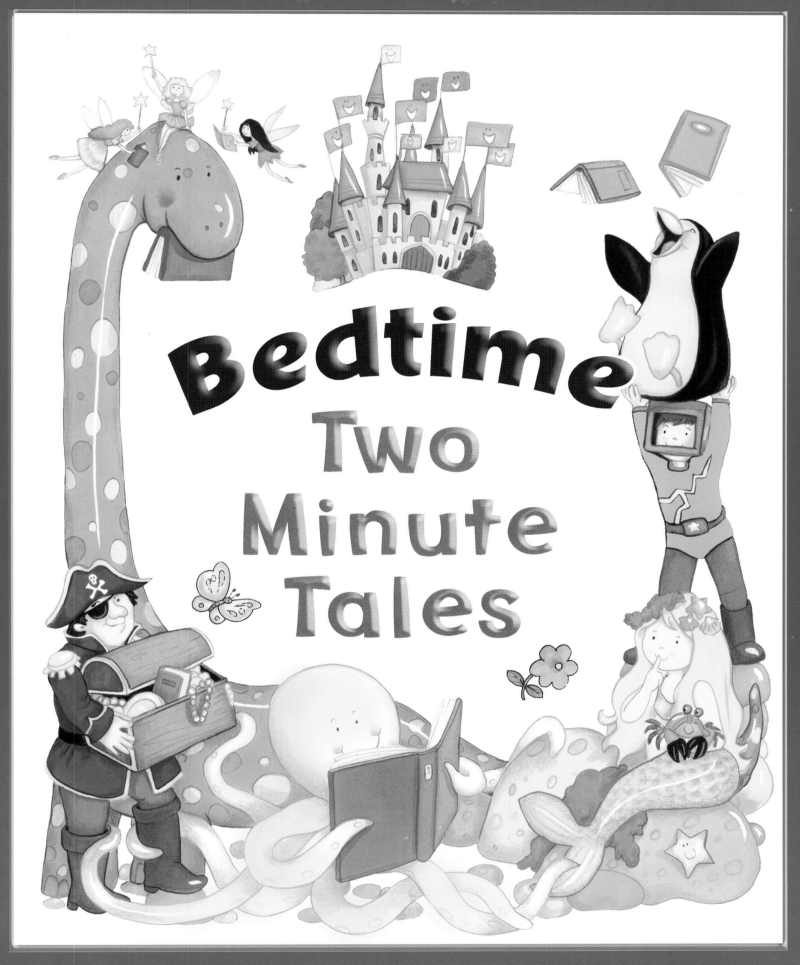

Bedtime Two Minute Tales

Written by Gill Guile

Brown Watson
ENGLAND

Mike's Mermaid

Mike lives by the seaside, in a pretty bungalow at the end of the beach. From his bedroom window he watches the waves splashing onto the sand and filling up the rock pools.

In summer the beach is covered with holiday makers, but in March the sands are empty and it becomes Mike's special place. Mike's mum watches him from the kitchen window as he explores the beach.

Mike likes to scramble over to the rock pools to see what the tide has washed in. Today he dangles his toes in the cold water and fishes for crabs and shrimps with his net. Under a big clump of seaweed he can see two beady eyes and the tip of a claw. A fat pink crab is hiding under there. Mike is trying to catch the crab when a head suddenly pops over the rocks. It's a little blonde girl, with shells and seaweed in her long wet hair.

The girl is called Marina and she seems to know an awful lot about the creatures in the pool. Mike and Marina spend hours collecting sea creatures in Mike's bucket, until his mummy calls him home for tea. Mike would like Marina to come for tea with him, but Marina giggles and says it would be impossible. She says it's time for her to go home too.

Mike wants to play with Marina again so she tells him to send her a message.

When Mike asks Marina for her address, she says he should write a note, put it in a bottle and throw it in the sea! Mike thinks that would be great fun, but surely the normal post would be better? Then he sees why she wants the message in a bottle. As she waves goodbye and dives back into the sea, he sees that Marina has a shiny green tail, covered in scales. 'She's a mermaid!' thinks Mike. 'I can't wait to tell my friends!'

Do you think they will believe him?

The Jungle Hospital

Leo Lion is in hospital with a broken leg, and he feels very sorry for himself. Nurse Elephant has put his injured leg in plaster and tucked him up in bed. Leo looks around at the other patients. In the next bed is Sally Snake with a sore throat. She is swaddled in thick, woolly scarves to keep her throat warm. Then there is Timmy Tiger who is covered in itchy, red spots and can't stop scratching.

Opposite him is Fenella Flamingo who has eaten something strange and has turned a bit green! No one is talking because they are all too busy feeling sorry for themselves. Suddenly the ward doors are flung open and Philip Frog trundles into the room in a wheelchair. Philip lost both his legs in an accident some time ago, but he is still as full of fun as he's ever been. Nurse Elephant has asked Philip to come in and try to cheer everyone up.

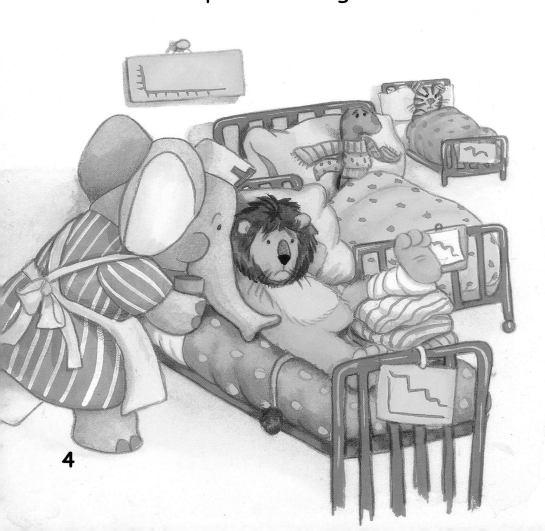

4

Philip spins around the room, talking to everyone and making them smile. Soon the room is buzzing with chatter and laughter. Philip stays for an hour, then leaves, promising to return the next day. Everyone feels so much better after his visit.

Nurse Elephant tells her patients that it is no use feeling sorry for themselves. There's always someone who's worse off than they are. They nod and smile and chat away for the rest of the day - and they can't wait to see Philip tomorrow!

Diana's Daisy Chain

Diana is always picking wild flowers for her Mummy. There are vases of wild flowers all over the house, making it look very pretty. Diana likes to look pretty too, so she runs into the garden to gather a basket full of daisies. With her fingernails she makes a small slit in each daisy stem, then threads the stems through each hole. Soon she has a really long daisy chain, which she winds around her arms and shoulders. Clever Diana, doesn't she look pretty?

Donny Digger

Little Donny Digger lives on a building site where a new supermarket is being built. Each day, Donny watches the big diggers preparing the ground. They scrape out great piles of earth and lumber back and forth across the building site, looking very important. Donny longs to join in but the big diggers tell him he's far too small and he'll just get in the way. Poor Donny!

Each of the Diggers has a big strong driver, but one day a new driver arrives who is much shorter than the others. It's difficult to find the right machine for Tommy, as most diggers are too big for him. When Tommy sees little Donny, he realises they suit each other perfectly. Donny and Tommy are very good at doing all the fiddly little jobs that are hard for bigger diggers, and that makes them a very happy pair.

The Tooth Fairy

Have you ever heard of the Tooth Fairy? She is a tiny little creature, only about the size of your thumb. When children's teeth fall out, the Tooth Fairy collects them.

The next time you lose a tooth, put it under your pillow when you go to bed and leave a little note with it. If you are lucky, the Tooth Fairy will take the tooth and leave a coin in its place.

The Tooth Fairy has to work very hard because there are hundreds of teeth to collect every night. She takes them back to a magic land where all the fairy folk live.

They use the teeth to build beautiful castles and palaces for the Fairy King and Queen. But the Tooth Fairy doesn't like bad teeth, she only picks clean, white baby teeth, which fall out by themselves. So don't forget to clean your teeth every day until they sparkle.

7

The Art Lesson

Today at school, the children are having an art lesson with Mrs Harper.

This is Elliott's favourite day of the week, because he's rather good at drawing and painting, and he'd love to be an artist when he grows up. Mrs Harper is having a competition to see who can paint the best picture of an Australian creature. It can be a bird, fish, insect or animal.

Mrs Harper lays out a huge pile of photographs for the children.

Nicki likes the colourful, red and yellow parrot; Chris wants to draw a big fierce looking shark; Beth picks a kangaroo with a long tail and powerful legs; and Vicki thinks it would be fun to paint a kookaburra. But Elliott just can't make up his mind. There are so many animals to choose from.

He doesn't want the pretty pink flamingo, the cute budgerigar, or the cuddly koala. He wants something that will catch the teacher's eye. Finally he finds the perfect creature. It's a very scary looking crocodile. He decides to paint the crocodile swimming in the water with its huge mouth open wide, showing rows of sharp pointed teeth. The children take the photographs back to their desks and collect some paper, brushes and paint pots.

Mrs Harper is very pleased with the children's paintings and hangs them all around the classroom. It's difficult for her to choose the winning picture because they are all so good. But then she comes to Elliott's painting and it is the best by far.

Mrs Harper gives first prize to Elliott. He wins a big bag of sweets, which he happily shares with all his classmates during break time.

Little Lost Zebra

Little Zebra is lost. He cannot find his mummy and there is no one else around. He begins to worry. There are three paths in front of him, but which is the way back home?

It is very hot so he follows the first track down to the river to have a drink. As he leans forwards a fearsome green head with rows of sharp white teeth explodes out of the water!

Little Zebra is terrified and bolts back to the clearing. Behind him Crocodile climbs out of the water and shakes himself dry.

'Maybe the second path is safer,' thinks Little Zebra. But as he trots along he hears a faint drumming sound. The noise gets closer and closer and louder and louder until the trees begin to shake and the ground trembles. Then a huge grey monster with flapping ears thunders across his path! Little Zebra races back to the clearing once more.

Behind him, Elephant crashes around in the bushes.

'This third path must be the way home,' sobs Little Zebra rushing along.

He stops suddenly as he hears a terrible roar. It is so loud that it makes his ears ring and his legs shake, so he gallops back as fast as he can.

'He's over here!' shouts Lion. 'He's in the clearing.'

Little Zebra is very scared.

He can hear the green sharp-toothed monster splashing up the first path. And the frightening ground-shaking monster is thundering up the second path. And the loud, hairy howling monster is roaring up the third path! HELP!

Then something lifts him high into the air. He squeezes his eyes shut and wishes Mummy was there but it's only Elephant with Crocodile and Lion.

Tired Little Zebra rides on Elephant's back all the way home to his mummy. What an exciting day he has had!

Spiky Solutions

Holly Hedgehog wakes up one sunny winter's day and pokes her spiky head out of the crisp pile of leaves she has been sleeping under. Holly has been asleep for two whole months now, although some years she sleeps for even longer. It is unusual for Holly to be awake during the day, but she thinks it might be nice to stretch her legs and go for a stroll!

On her way across the garden, Holly spots Ricky Robin flitting to and fro with scraps of bread and bacon rind in his beak.

He is collecting food for a party at the oak tree at one o'clock, but it is already five minutes to one and Ricky is worried that his friends will arrive before he is ready. He can only carry one scrap of food in his beak on each journey and Holly notices that he is very tired. Then she thinks of a clever way to help.

She curls up into a spiky ball and rolls around the lawn. All the bits of food stick to her prickles. She does look funny!

Holly collects all the food and trots across the grass to the oak tree just as the guests are arriving. Martha Mouse and Scarlet Squirrel have come together, Belinda Bluebird has flown and finally Cyrill Snail slithered across the garden slowly. Ricky Robin is delighted and invites Holly to join them.

Holly has a lovely afternoon with all her friends, but as the sun begins to sink in the sky, it becomes very cold again. Holly suddenly feels very sleepy now, so she says goodbye to everyone and shuffles back across the lawn to her cosy nest of leaves. As the last leaf settles over her head, Holly gives a gentle snore. She is already fast asleep! What a wonderful day she has had.

No place like home

There are some creatures that love snow, and the colder it gets, the better they like it.

Peggy Penguin lives in the Antarctic, which is down at the bottom of the earth and is a very chilly place to live. Everywhere is white and covered in snow. It is almost always Winter here.

Peggy lives on an iceberg in the sea with a large group of other penguins. Every day they swim and catch fish in the freezing waters.

Every few weeks, large ships, bulging with tourists, stop at Peggy's iceberg to photograph the penguins. These people come from much hotter lands, which Peggy longs to visit because she is tired of being cold. One day Peggy manages to stow away on a ship bound for Italy. She hides amongst boxes and crates until the long journey is finally over and the boat docks.

The sun blazes fiercely over bright flowers, green trees, noisy people and smelly cars.

14

Peggy is hot, hungry and very homesick. Thoughts of the Antarctic fill her head and she longs for the cool, quiet calm of the iceberg. She hurries back to her hiding place amid the boxes and crates and waits for the ship to sail back home. When she finally gets home, the other penguins want to hear all about her travels. Peggy never dreams about other countries now because she knows, there's no place like home!

The Scary Scarecrow

Mark, Victoria and Sophie are having a competition to see who can make the best scarecrow. Mark would love to win but he's only four and his eight year old twin sisters seem much smarter than him. They make their scarecrows in Farmer Ben's field, and he will give a prize for the best one.

Victoria has nearly finished. Her scarecrow has a lovely pink scarf and a floppy hat, which she covers with bows and feathers.

Sophie's wears an old top hat, with matching gloves that she found in the dressing-up box. She has drawn a big smile on its pumpkin face. The two scarecrows look fabulous! Mark looks at his effort, an old brush with a scarf tied round it, and decides to go home as he's sure he won't win. Back home he draws an angry face to show how he feels. He thinks it will make a good mask, but when he puts it on it scares the cat. This gives Mark an idea.

Mark races back to the field and ties his mask to the brush, just as Farmer Ben arrives to judge their efforts. The farmer thinks the twins' scarecrows are great but he knows they won't scare the birds away, which is, of course, why we have scarecrows! So Mark's scary scarecrow wins the prize - a big bag of juicy apples, which he happily shares with his sisters! Then he goes home to draw another face. A happy smiley one this time!

Olly to the Rescue

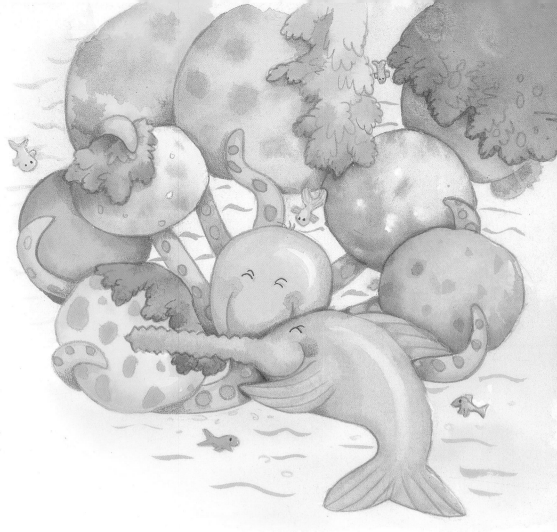

Olly Octopus has moved to a new home in the ocean. He is quite a shy octopus and finds it hard to make new friends. Poor Olly is feeling rather lonely.

One day as he is swimming along the ocean floor, he hears a cry for help. Sally Swordfish is trapped under a pile of heavy boulders and Sammy Shark and Daisy Dolphin are trying to push the rocks away to free her. As soon as one rock is pushed aside another slides down in its place.

It is a hopeless task and Olly sees that Sally is really upset. What Sammy and Daisy need is someone to hold back each rock as it is pushed to one side. They need a few extra hands, and guess what? Olly has eight! Sammy and Daisy begin clearing the rocks one by one until Olly is holding on to eight big boulders. Finally Sally can escape. She shoots out of the rocks and gives Olly a big hug. Now he's a hero and everyone wants to be his friend.

Alien Invasion

James longs to be a spaceman. He has lots of books about astronauts and his bedroom walls are covered with pictures of planets and rockets. He loves make-believe games about space.

One day, he runs into the garden wearing a homemade space suit, ready to tackle any fierce monsters. James doesn't know it yet, but today he's going to meet some real aliens!

Out in deepest, darkest space, an alien spaceship approaches our solar system.

It has been travelling for many years, looking for a new planet to live on. The creatures on the ship built the largest machine that has ever been seen on their planet. Inside, there is a city with roads, gardens and room for them and all their animals and crops too. Now the captain thinks he has found a planet that looks very nice.

The captain lands the ship near a lake, in an area covered with tall, green plants. The aliens climb down the ladder to look around. Suddenly, the sky darkens and deafening thunder shakes the ground. Terrified aliens scramble up the ladder to safety. This planet is much too scary afterall!

James is racing round the garden, fighting pretend aliens, when he senses something whizz past his nose and land next to a puddle in the long grass.

James kneels down to take a closer look and sees a metal object, the size of an apple pip, with tiny insect-like creatures pouring out of it. As soon as his shadow falls over them, they stream back in. Then the little metal pip shoots past him, way up into the sky. 'What on Earth was that?' wonders James, as he goes back to his game. Well we know, don't we?

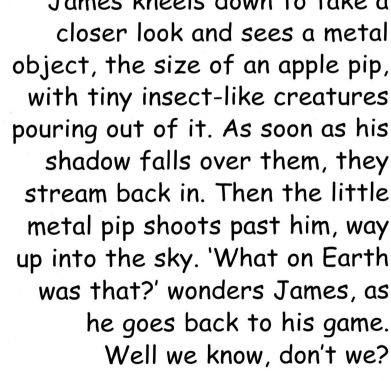

Wendy's Wood

Wendy looks out of her bedroom window towards the wood at the bottom of the garden. All the leaves in the wood have fallen on the ground during winter, so it's difficult for Wendy to recognise all the different trees. Her big brother, William, says there are lots of clues in the wood and offers to help. Wendy runs off to find her wellies. William tells her to look for an oak tree first.

Wendy knows acorns come from oak trees, so she looks high up above her for some squirrels, which eat acorns. She quickly spots a couple and follows them to a sturdy tree with a dark, rough trunk. Under the tree she finds lots of old, dried leaves. 'Found one!' she laughs. She pops a leaf in her pocket. Next she looks for old conkers, which are the fruit of the horse chestnut tree. She often plays conkers with her friends so she should easily recognise this tree.

William says horse chestnut leaves have five to seven fingers. She soon spots one and pockets it, then she rushes off to find a sycamore. They have squarish leaves with three to seven fat fingers. William says sycamores have smooth tree bark and seeds like helicopers! When Wendy finds a seed, she drops it and watches as it spins slowly down to the ground. The silver birch is easy to spot because of its white bark. The holly tree is easy too with its Christmassy leaf.

Soon, Wendy's pockets are bulging with dried leaves. When she gets home she traces round the leaves and labels each picture. Then she sticks them in a scrapbook, ready to take to school on Monday. William thinks Wendy's teacher would like to see the scrapbook. The teacher thinks the book is wonderful and gives Wendy a gold star! Later, all the children in Wendy's class are taken on a nature ramble and they have fun making their own leaf scrapbooks. Why don't you try it?

oak

horse chestnut

silver birch

sycamore

holly

Sally Spider

Sally Spider lives in the wood, half way up a sycamore tree, with lots of spider friends.

Each day they make new webs by spinning and weaving threads of silk into wonderful webs. Spiders live in their webs but they are also sticky traps for flies, which is how spiders catch their food.

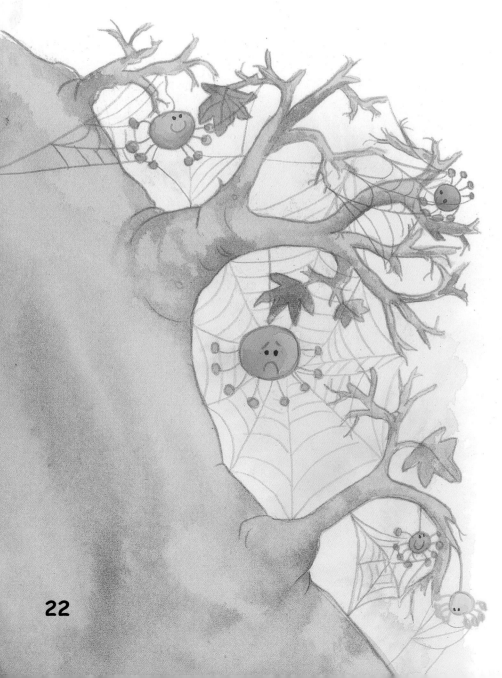

Because Sally is a very quick weaver, she usually finishes her web by lunchtime and then has nothing else to do for the rest of the day. In summer there are lots of other creatures around to chat to, but in chilly winter everyone comes out of their burrows and nests just long enough to find some food, then they rush back to their warm homes.

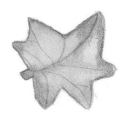

Sally thinks that if she could keep her friends warm, they might stay around for a chat. She knows exactly what to do. All afternoon she spins and weaves until she has a pile of long, thin webs. The other spiders are puzzled because these are the strangest webs they've ever seen! 'Whatever is she up to?' they wonder. The next day they find out.

As Ruby Robin flies past, Sally calls out to her. 'Would you like a nice warm scarf, Ruby?'

Ruby is delighted and chats for ages! A little later on, Henry Hare hops by, and Sally asks, 'Would you like a nice warm scarf, Henry?'

Henry is so pleased he stays til teatime. Now everybody wants a scarf and Sally is never bored. She spins and chats all day long!

Fashion Fairy

Little Fairy Lucy flutters around the snow-blanketed garden. I wonder what she is looking for? She looks very pretty in her winter clothes. She's wearing a tiny pair of green gloves made out of moss; beautiful, soft mushroom-skin boots; cobweb tights and a winter heather dress. Her clothes keep her nice and warm but her head feels rather cold. So she is searching for a winter hat.

Most of the plants and trees in the garden have gone to sleep over winter. The holly bush looks fresh and bright with its red berries, but it would make a very prickly hat! Lucy spots an acorn shell under the oak tree. It fits quite well, but Lucy suspects it probably looks a bit odd and it keeps slipping over her eyes! Finally she sees the perfect hat, poking through the snow in the rockery. It's a snowdrop. When Lucy shows it to her fairy friends, they will all want one too!

Bunny and Honey

Jamie has two cuddly pet rabbits, who live in a hutch at the bottom of his garden. Bunny is a black and white rabbit. He is full of mischief and is always trying to escape. Honey is a large, gentle lop-eared rabbit, who just wants to be cuddled. Each morning before school, Jamie cleans out the rabbit hutch and gives them clean water and fresh food.

This morning Jamie hasn't closed the hutch door properly, so Bunny pushes it open with his nose and escapes into the garden. Jamie chases after him but it's too late, Bunny has disappeared. Mummy promises to help look for him after school, so Jamie locks Honey away and hopes Bunny doesn't get too cold outside.

Bunny is very pleased with himself. He nibbles some grass and then goes off to explore the garden.

As the day goes on, Bunny gets hungry and he remembers the juicy carrots and lettuce Jamie brought him that morning. He feels cold and he remembers the fresh warm hay in the hutch. He gets lonely, and worst of all he misses Honey. At four o'clock when Jamie gets home, the first thing he sees is a very unhappy rabbit, huddling next to the hutch. As Jamie opens the door, Bunny rushes in and snuggles next to Honey. Bunny has had his little adventure and he will be quite happy to stay with Honey in future.

The Forgetful Koala

Kelly Koala is always in trouble because she finds it so hard to remember things.

She forgets to tell Mummy Koala when she goes out to play, she forgets to put her watch on, she forgets her lunch and her homework. Sometimes she even forgets to go to school!

Every morning when she gets out of bed, Kelly knows she is going to forget something important, but she doesn't know what to do about it.

26

Katie Kangaroo feels very sorry for Kelly and tries to think of a way to help her remember some of the most important things.

She finds a little notepad and pencil in a cupboard at home and takes it round to Kelly's house. Now Kelly can write down everything that she needs to remember. 'What a good idea,' thinks Kelly. But she's so absent minded that she keeps forgetting where she has left the notepad!

Katie thinks this is really funny because she knows an absolutely perfect place for Kelly to keep her notepad and pencil. Like Katie, and lots of other Australian animals, Kelly is a marsupial.

Female marsupials have a little pouch or pocket near their tummies. This is where the mummies keep their babies when they are small and it is the perfect place for Kelly to keep her notepad. She hardly ever forgets anything now!

27

Fergie's Homework

Fergie Frog has some very hard homework to do today. Maths really isn't his favourite subject, he'd much rather be playing with his brothers and sisters. Fergie can count all the way up to twenty, but when he has to add and take away numbers, it becomes much too tricky. Mummy Frog sees him struggling with his homework and thinks of a simpler way to do his sums.

Mummy calls all the family over to the pond. It is a big family and altogether Fergie has nine brothers and six sisters! Mummy is going to use all the children to help Fergie with his sums.

This is the first sum...
7 + 5 – 3 =

Mummy sends seven of Fergie's brothers over to a lily pad. They splash across the water, climb out and stand in line. Then she sends five of the sisters to join them.

28

Mummy tells three of the little frogs to jump back in the pond. 'Now Fergie, count how many frogs are left on the lily pad,' she says.

Fergie counts to nine. It's such an easy way to do maths homework! Fergie sends the frogs back and forth across the pond until all his sums are finished. Everyone enjoys themselves and Fergie manages to play with his family and do his homework correctly!

Tomorrow's homework is going to be geography, I wonder if that will be fun too!

Snail Trail

It has been raining all morning, so all the slugs, snails and worms have been playing out in the downpour. They love wet weather. Now the sun is shining fiercely and they all slither back to their damp hiding places. All except Suzy Snail. Daddy Snail decides to track her down. It's quite easy because snails leave a slimy trail behind them. He soon spots her climbing up a car tyre. Not a very sensible place to be, thinks Dad, as he calls her back. They slip and slide home just in time for tea.

29

The Golden Tree

Stories of Wilfrid Wizard, Winifrid Witch and their golden tree have stopped many brave men from venturing into the Wild Wood. None who have entered the wood in search of the tree have ever returned, and so the legend lives on. Anthony lives in a village just outside the Wild Wood. He plans to find his way to the wizard and witch's cottage and bring back a branch of the golden tree.

The branch should bring him fame and fortune, and then he will be able to ask the beautiful Miranda to marry him. One sunny day, Anthony rides off into the wood. He is gone for many weeks and Miranda worries that she will never see him again. When Anthony finally emerges from the wood he is very tired and miserable, but everyone wants to hear his story. Anthony tells them that he searched the woods for weeks and weeks before he came across a derelict old cottage.

The building had not been used for centuries. He knew that the witch and wizard had once lived there because inside he found old spell books along with mysterious looking jars and a broken cauldron. In the garden Anthony uncovered a cracked headstone where Wilfrid and Winifrid had been buried hundreds of years ago. Next to the headstone stood a tree covered in golden blossom, but there was nothing special about this tree. It was just an ordinary yellow laburnum.

Filled with disappointment, Anthony found his way back home. He didn't think Miranda would want to marry him now, but he was wrong. Miranda thought Anthony was the bravest person she had ever met and wanted to marry him and live in the derelict cottage. And because it was now safe to enter the wood, they could make a living hunting there. So Anthony and Miranda lived happily ever after in the wizard and witch's lovely old cottage.

Charlie the Clown

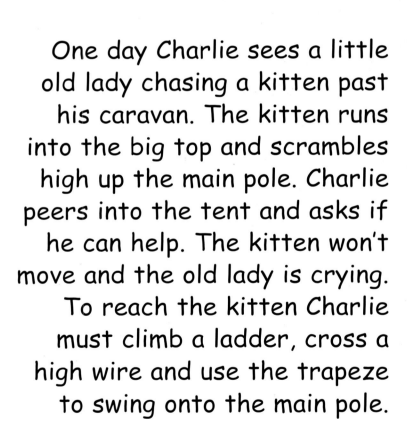

Charlie's family have been clowns for as long as anyone can remember and it is expected that Charlie will be a clown too. The trouble is, Charlie would rather be a high wire or trapeze artiste, but no one will listen to him. So whenever he can find the time he practices balancing and walking across his mum's washing line.

One day Charlie sees a little old lady chasing a kitten past his caravan. The kitten runs into the big top and scrambles high up the main pole. Charlie peers into the tent and asks if he can help. The kitten won't move and the old lady is crying. To reach the kitten Charlie must climb a ladder, cross a high wire and use the trapeze to swing onto the main pole.

Charlie's parents arrive just as he's about to cross the high wire. They shout at him to turn back but Charlie is concentrating too hard to hear them. He's nearly there now! Just half a metre to go, and yes, he makes it across the wire safely. Then he reaches for the trapeze and with a huge jump he launches himself high into the air. They all hold their breaths as he somersaults and lands neatly next to the little kitten.

Charlie scoops the kitten into his arms and jumps off the platform onto the safety net. Everybody cheers. The little old lady says Charlie is a hero and can't thank him enough. Charlie's Mum and Dad are so impressed with Charlie's skills that they tell him he can start training for the high wire if that's what he wants. Charlie can't wait!

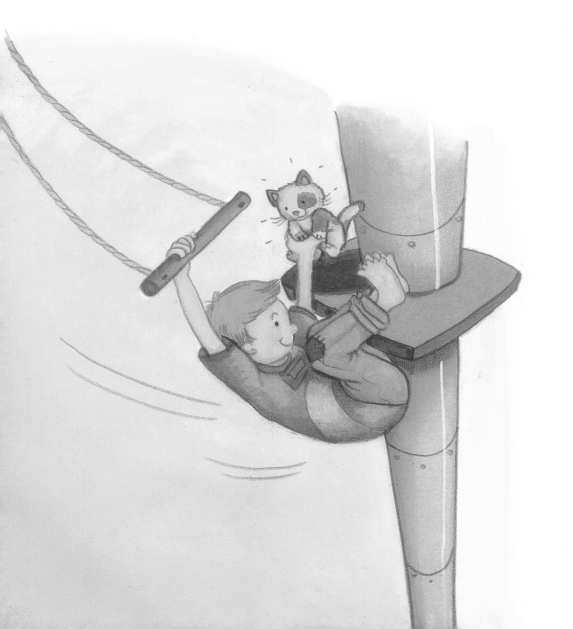

A Bad Spell

In the jungle, the animals are playing Blind Man's Bluff, while Little Fairy is fluttering in and out of the trees. What is she looking for? Monkey knows, because he found it earlier that morning. It is a book of very magical spells and, being naughty, he has decided to try one of the spells out on his friends.

The animals blindfold Lion. He has to catch them and guess who each of them is. EASY!

Elephant has flappy ears and a long trunk; Giraffe is tall with a long neck; and Tortoise is so slow!

Then Monkey casts his spell:
'Your shapes I'll change
to something strange.
That flappy ear will disappear,
And what came last
will now be fast!'

Lion catches the first animal. It seems to have small ears, a tiny nose and wrinkly skin. Who can it be?

The next animal has short legs, a short neck and a long tail. Who can this be?

The third animal is impossible to catch because it's moving too fast! Who can this be?

Lion is very confused and takes off his blindfold to see what is happening. All his friends have changed shape. Behind them, high up in the banana tree, he can see Monkey laughing so hard that he nearly loses his balance! Lion opens his mouth to roar at Monkey but all that comes out is a tiny squeak!

Little Fairy sees Monkey clutching her spell book and realises what he's done. She is very cross and grabs the book from Monkey.

'Hear my spell you naughty ape, I'll turn you yellow and change your shape. You must be good and stop being bad, Or my spell will last and you'll be sad!'

In a puff of pink smoke, they all change back, except for Monkey who has suddenly changed into a giant banana! He feels very foolish. The spell will wear off by bedtime, but every time he is naughty he will turn back into a big yellow banana!

I think he will be a very good monkey from now on, don't you?

Fat Cat

Tommy's cat is getting fat. She seems to get rounder everyday! Tommy tells his Mum that he's worried Fliss might burst if she keeps on growing. Mummy tells Tommy not to worry because Fliss isn't being greedy. She has lots of babies growing in her tummy, and they could be born at any time. When Tommy gently strokes Fliss's tummy, he can feel the babies moving inside.

One day, when Tommy gets back from school, his Mummy calls him into the kitchen. He discovers Fliss surrounded by eight mewing bundles of fur. All the kittens have their eyes closed. When the kittens are old enough to leave their mum, they will all go to good homes, but Tommy pleads to be able to keep one. Mummy agrees and Tommy chooses a little black one with a white mark on her nose. He decides to call her Floss. Isn't Tommy lucky!

Digging Dennis

Dennis the Dog loves digging holes for his bones. He digs lots of holes all over old Mrs Mottram's garden. Mrs Mottram sighs when she sees her ruined flowerbeds. It will take all day to replant the flowers and she still has the vegetable patch to dig over. Her old bones are aching before she even picks up the spade! Then she has an idea. She gathers up the flowers in a basket, and putting on her hat and coat, she heads off to the florist shop.

The lady at the florist is happy to buy Mrs Mottram's flowers. She can make beautiful flower arrangements to sell in her shop. With the money she receives, Mrs Mottram buys some sausages for tea and a dozen large marrow bones. She gets home and tosses the bones into the vegetable patch. Dennis the Dog is happy to bury the bones, which helpfully digs over the soil. Now it's easy to plant the seeds! It's soon teatime and Mrs Mottram has a big plate of sausage and mash. I think she's earned it, don't you?

Alphabet Animals

Wise old owl teaches in Bluebell Wood School every morning.

Today, Owl wants his pupils to name one creature for every letter of the alphabet so that they can write a poem. Each of the eight pupils has three letters.

Bunny has ABC, Fox has DEF, Hen has GHI, Kingfisher has JKL, Mouse has MNO, Squirrel has PRS, Vole has TUV, Worm has WYZ and Owl has the two most difficult letters, Q and X.

Everyone makes their list, then Owl helps them with the rhyme.

A is an ALLIGATOR,
a green, scary brute.

B is a BUNNY,
long-eared and cute.

C is for CAT,
with lovely soft fur.

D is a DOG,
who can bark but not purr.

E is for ELEPHANT,
with huge trunk and ears.

F is the FOX,
that Bunny here fears.

G for GIRAFFES,
with long spotty necks.

H is that HEN,
who scratches and pecks.

I for IGUANA,
a scaley reptile.

J for the JACKAL
who's often hostile.

K is KINGFISHER,
who's sitting right here.

L is a LION,
whom I know you all fear.

M is for MOUSE,
so dainty and sweet.

N is for NEWT,
with little webbed feet.

O is for OCTOPUS,
with tentacles, eight!

P is for PENGUIN,
we all think they're great!

Q is a QUEEN BEE,
surrounded by honey.

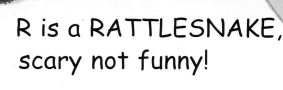

R is a RATTLESNAKE,
scary not funny!

S is for SQUIRREL,
a collector of nuts.

T is the TIGER,
who'll be after your guts!

U is the UNICORN,
made up, not true.

V is for VOLE,
sitting right next to you.

W is WORM,
in that hole by my tree.

X, X-RAY FISH
that live in the sea.

Y is a YAK,
a peculiar sight!

And Z is for ZEBRA,
with stripes, black and white.

The Lost Wellies

James lives on a farm. It's often quite muddy so there are always lots of Wellington boots to be found - and lost. James always seems to lose the left boot and today he discovers that, yet again, one left boot is missing. Dad is cross and refuses to buy another new pair, so James must borrow one of Dad's spares, (which are too enormous to walk in), or borrow one of Mum's, (which are pink), or he must search again to find the lost one. He chooses the last option!

James looks everywhere until there is only the duck pond left. As he searches through the reeds, he sees his blue boot hidden near the water's edge. Bending down to retrieve it, he finds a nest of eggs inside the boot! James doesn't know what to do, as he can't disturb the nest. Then he spots something bobbing up and down near the lily pads. It's the red boot he lost last month. Hurray! Now he can wear the old red boot with the blue boot he has at home.

Rainy Day Puppets

It's raining today and Roseanna and Francesca are trying to think of something to do. Mummy asks them to look under their beds to see what they can find. Between them, they discover three odd socks and an old black glove. The girls put their finds on the kitchen table, where Mummy has laid out felt tips, buttons, glue, scissors and some scraps of material.

Mummy helps the girls to sew on button eyes and draw noses and mouths on the socks. Then, using the glue, they stick multicoloured strips on them to make hair. The hand puppets look really cool and Roseanna and Francesca can't wait to show them to all of their friends.

'But what shall we make with this old glove?' asks Roseanna.

Mummy draws two cross-looking eyes and sticks them on the glove. The children still do not know what it is supposed to be.

'Put the glove on, Francesca,' says Mummy. Now the girls see what it is: a five-legged spider! 'Cool!' they laugh.

Wally Warthog's Wish

Wally Warthog lives in the forest. He is covered in bristly, black hair and has a lumpy, bumpy sort of skin and a pair of long, sharp tusks either side of a podgy little snout. Wally wishes he was handsome and worries that the other forest animals are laughing at him because he is so ugly. He tries to keep away from everyone and that makes him a very lonely warthog.

Wally sees Freddy Fox and wishes he had beautiful red fur. He sees Sally Squirrel and wishes he had a fantastic, bushy tail like she does. He sees Milly and Molly Mouse and wishes he had a dainty little nose like they do. Then he sees someone new to the forest, although there is something strangely familiar about her. She has the same shuffling walk as Wally. The same gleaming white tusks. Identical strong, bristly hair and a cute little tail!

She is ambling along, pushing her snout through the leaves and looking for something tasty to eat. When she spots him, she smiles at Wally and blushes prettily. Her name is Winnie Warthog and she thinks Wally is the most handsome creature she has ever seen! Wally thinks Winnie is beautiful too. For the first time in their lives, the two warthogs feel happy with the way they look. They decide they were made for each other and live happily ever after.

Daydreaming Darren

Darren is a daydreamer. Instead of paying attention at school, he imagines being a fighter pilot or a famous lawyer; a pop star or maybe a television personality. Anything but pay attention to his lessons. One day, a famous television sports presenter visits the school to talk to the children about careers.

The guest asks the children if any of them have thought about a career as a sports presenter.

Darren's hand shoots up. The man asks him if there is a particular sport that he is good at. Darren shakes his head, he spends too much of his time daydreaming to practise much sport. The man asks if Darren is good at English or Drama. But again, Darren shakes his head, he is far too busy daydreaming to do his English homework, or maths, science, geography, or anything really.

The presenter says that if the children want to have interesting careers, the most important step is to work hard and pay attention when they are at school.

Darren thinks maybe he should concentrate in his lessons in future because he really would like to be famous like the guest. He is suddenly aware that it is very quiet in the classroom and looks up to find the lesson is over and everyone has left. Oops, Darren has been daydreaming again!

A Change for Caterpillar

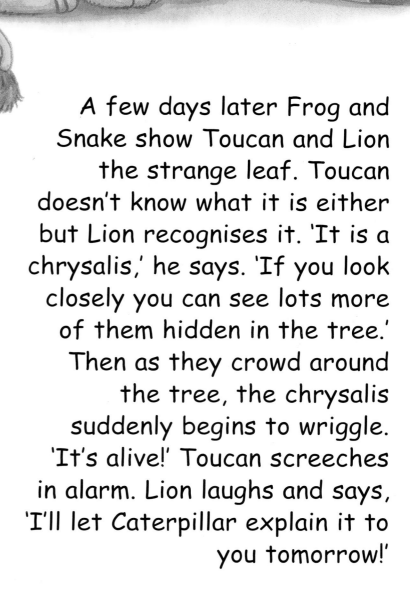

Each morning Snake and Frog follow the same path to the river. One day, as they are passing the big tree where Caterpillar lives, Snake notices something strange hanging from a low branch.

'What do you think that is?' he asks. 'Well it looks like a leaf, but it doesn't match the other leaves,' says Frog. 'Perhaps Caterpillar knows.' But Caterpillar was nowhere to be found!

A few days later Frog and Snake show Toucan and Lion the strange leaf. Toucan doesn't know what it is either but Lion recognises it. 'It is a chrysalis,' he says. 'If you look closely you can see lots more of them hidden in the tree.' Then as they crowd around the tree, the chrysalis suddenly begins to wriggle. 'It's alive!' Toucan screeches in alarm. Lion laughs and says, 'I'll let Caterpillar explain it to you tomorrow!'

The next day they gather around the tree. The chrysalis wriggles and shakes until its little sack splits and then out crawls a beautiful butterfly. She flutters around the animals' heads. 'Hi guys, I'm back!' she squeaks. Snake is puzzled. 'I know that voice, but you're not Caterpillar!'

Butterfly smiles. 'For the first part of our lives we are caterpillars, and for the rest we are butterflies. It is still me.' Around them, hundreds of butterflies emerge. Toucan laughs. 'It's all very confusing, but now I can race you to the river!' And they fly off with their friends racing after them.

The Greedy Pirate

Captain Rich Pickens is a very greedy pirate. He captures ships and sails away with all their gold and jewels. But his pirate ship isn't very big, and gradually, the hold, the deck and each of the rooms has filled up with treasure. The pirate crew are worried that their ship may sink, and ask the captain if they can go home, but greedy Captain Pickens doesn't know when to stop! Then, one breezy April afternoon, the lookout spies a galleon on the horizon. The pirates race after the ship and capture it.

The ship is full of precious jewels and coins but the captured captain warns the pirates that their ship will not be able to withstand the extra weight. The crew agree with their prisoner, but Captain Pickens will not listen and orders his men to haul a giant treasure chest on board. The ship begins to groan under its heavy burden. Then, quietly at first, there is the sound of splintering wood and nails popping. The crew realise the ship is breaking up and throw the chest into the sea. But it is too late so they rapidly abandon ship.

All except Captain Pickens, who refuses to leave. He is soon ankle deep in water! The captain of the other ship is back in charge and he offers to help the men if they give up piracy and come and work for him. The crew are happy to agree as they have had more than enough piracy now. Captain Pickens refuses to join them, so he is sent off in a little rowing boat.

He'll probably spend the rest of his days rowing around the site of his sunken ship, trying to work out ways of salvaging his treasure! Some people never learn!

Monster Feast

The giant troll in Monster Castle is having a cookery competition and the castle is heaving with hundreds of fairies and witches, all hoping to win the huge chest of gold, which is first prize.

Fairies and witches don't really get on, so from the towering, black castle, you can hear voices screeching and squabbling, and pots and pans clanging and banging, and clouds of steam, smoke and stars pouring out of the kitchen windows!

One by one most of the cooks are eliminated, until only two finalists remain. These are Fairy Nuf and Witch Wayupp. They bring their final three dishes to the long table in the Great Hall.

Fairy Nuf has made moonshine soup, followed by flutterby wing salad, and for pudding she has made sunlight syllabub, served in a bluebell cup. Delicious! Witch Wayupp has cooked bats' ears in filo pastry, followed by a main course of fried toads in a red wine sauce, and finally there is a magnificent tower of frog spawn profiteroles! Not so delicious!

Suddenly, just as everyone is wondering which meal the troll will choose, he grabs Fairy Nuf and Witch Wayupp and crams them both into his mouth! The witch jams her broom between his jaws and Fairy Nuf quickly casts a spell, which shrinks the troll to the size of a spider. He scuttles away into a nearby mouse hole. The terrified witch and fairy realise that teamwork has saved them from a horrible fate and from that day on, all the witches and fairies remain good friends

Untidy Tiger

Trevor Tiger is a very untidy creature. He can never find a thing, and his den is a clutter of rubbish, books and broken toys. One day his friends call round to see if Trevor will play football with them, but he simply cannot find his boots! Three hours later, Trevor finds the boots hidden beneath a pile of clothes, but when he reaches the field, everyone has gone home! If only Trevor's den had not been such a mess! From now on he's going to be a very tidy tiger!

Timmy the Tug Boat

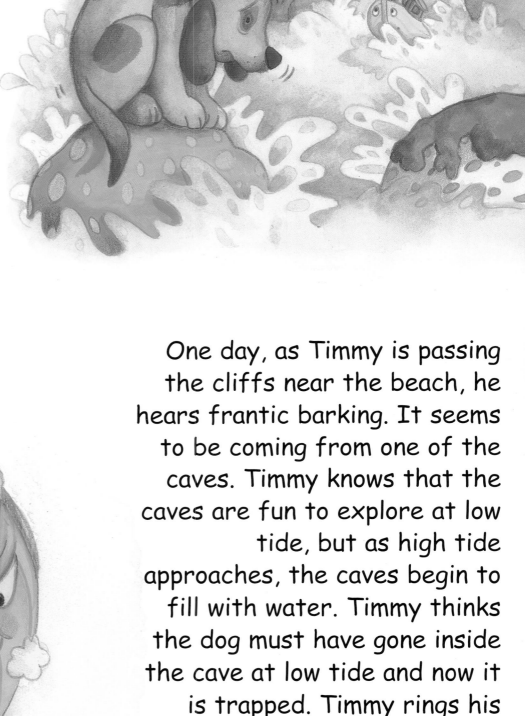

Timmy is a little tugboat with big ideas. He wants to be a lifeboat and rescue people in danger. But the big lifeboats laugh at Timmy and tell him he is far too small to be of any help. They look so important and busy that Timmy tries to keep out of their way. He spends most days just chugging up and down the coast, keeping a look out for anyone in distress.

One day, as Timmy is passing the cliffs near the beach, he hears frantic barking. It seems to be coming from one of the caves. Timmy knows that the caves are fun to explore at low tide, but as high tide approaches, the caves begin to fill with water. Timmy thinks the dog must have gone inside the cave at low tide and now it is trapped. Timmy rings his bell to alert the lifeboats and nervously waits outside.

Two big strong lifeboats arrive within minutes.

'Stand back, Timmy. You can leave this to us,' they call. The boats take turns to try and squeeze through the narrow cave opening, but they are far too wide. The dog sounds really frightened now and Timmy worries the rising sea might soon sweep it away.

Timmy decides he must help and launches himself through the opening. He reaches the stranded dog, seconds before a big wave sweeps into the cave, covering the very rock the dog had been clinging to. When Timmy emerges from the cave with the grateful dog, it's to a hero's welcome from the big lifeboats. From now on, brave little Timmy will patrol alongside the big boats, because who knows when they may need him next!

Jungle Sports Day

Today is Sports Day for the jungle animals and the first event is the three-legged race. All the animals form a line: Giraffe, Rhino and Elephant are strapped together; Lion, Zebra and Crocodile are also tied together; and Tortoise, Sloth and Turtle form the third group. The bigger animals snigger when they see this little trio, they don't think there will be any competition from them!

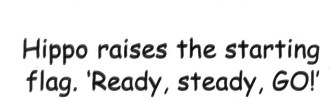

Hippo raises the starting flag. 'Ready, steady, GO!'

As they whiz past the coconut palms, Elephant's group are just in front. They round a corner and head towards a tangle of jungle vines. 'Duck!' cries Rhino. But it's too late, Giraffe's neck becomes entangled in the vines and they grind to a halt. Lion, Zebra and Crocodile surge ahead but they don't see the huge, sticky spider's web which is stretched across the track.

Far behind everyone else, the final little trio plod on. They are very surprised when they overtake Elephant's group, frantically trying to pull Giraffe free. They are even more surprised when they pass Lion's group, all caught up in a giant, sticky web. But they simply can't believe it when they hobble past the finishing post in first place. Turtle, Sloth and Tortoise are the winners and they receive a wonderful trophy. Well done to the slow coaches!

The Unhaunted House

Rosie Rat is a timid little creature and all her school friends tease her, so she thinks of a plan to make them think she's brave. At the end of an overgrown lane, close to the wood, stands a tumbledown old house that everyone thinks is haunted. Rosie's school friends are daring each other to spend a night in the old house, but no one is brave enough - except for Rosie!

The other animals can hardly believe that timid little Rosie will go through with it, but they walk with her to the house that night and wave goodbye. The heavy front door creaks open and Rosie disappears inside. As she walks through the house the floorboards squeak and groan. Outside, Rosie's school friends are so scared by the spooky noises that they all run home to bed!

Rosie climbs the rotting staircase and tiptoes into the main bedroom. As she climbs onto the old bed she can hear slow footsteps following up the stairs behind her. Then the bedroom door creaks open. 'Hi, Aunty Ruth and Uncle Ross,' says Rosie. 'Please may I stay for the night?' Rosie's aunt and uncle live here in this quiet old house. Rosie can't wait to see her friends in the morning. She knows they'll never tease her about being timid again!

The Sad Little Starfish

Little Starfish lives in the ocean with all the other sea creatures. He is surrounded by crabs, fish, shrimp, sharks and jellyfish, but he'd really like to see someone just like himself. Each night he searches the sea bed, but he can never seem to find another starfish. One night, the waves are much stronger than usual and Little Starfish is washed up onto a beach.

He crawls towards an outcrop of rocks, hoping to find a quiet rock pool to spend the night in. By the time he reaches the rocks he is exhausted, and lies quietly on a stone, gazing up at the night. The sky is awash with twinkling stars, which look a bit like he does! As he is smiling up at the stars, he hears something splashing out of the rock pool. It's another little starfish! She also watches the stars at night and she is lonely too. Now they have met, they will live happily ever after.

Tough Tommy

Tommy is a big, blue truck. He is very strong and can carry almost anything. Last week he drove two enormous elephants from one zoo to another, fifty miles away. It's all in a day's work for Tommy the truck.

Tommy likes the way that everyone looks up to him but he has a secret fear. Tommy worries that one day he might have to use his horn.

Tommy would love a great big booming horn but his just makes an embarrassing little squeak! Tommy can't bear the thought of everyone laughing at him.

To avoid using his horn, Tommy will not drive anywhere that is busy. He drives through the quiet countryside where he's unlikely to meet anyone, but this makes his journeys much longer than they need to be.

Today is Tommy's birthday and he is exactly one year old. There is going to be a big birthday party this afternoon and all the other trucks from Tommy's yard will be there. But there is one little problem. Tommy still has one last delivery to make and if he goes the long way round, he will be late for his own party. Poor Tommy, whatever should he do now?

The other trucks don't know why Tommy is so sad but to cheer him up they decide to give him their present before he leaves. He rips off the paper and can't believe his luck when he opens the box. It is a big, shiny, fabulously noisy horn! Tommy is delighted. Now he can go the shorter routes and use his horn as much as he likes. He races off with the final load and is soon back in time to enjoy his party.

Clever Miss Snake

It is Saturday morning and Fenella Flamingo, Gail Gazelle, Jillie Giraffe and Hetty Hippo are going to their ballet lesson. They are very excited because this is the last rehearsal before tonight's big show. They have had to leave Ziggy Zebra behind because she has a bad cold and they are feeling a little worried because Ziggy takes care of all the jobs that need doing off stage.

The friends want everything to run smoothly as all their families will be seated in the front row. Miss Snake, the ballet teacher, can see how nervous the four friends are and feels sorry for them. She thinks of a way to get all the jobs running smoothly.

Miss Snake tells the class that she needs someone to do some very important jobs as well as dancing. Nobody wants to give up all their dance routines so each dancer has one small job to do, while the others dance.

They each take turns to move the scenery, control the lights, take charge of the curtains and keep the music playing while Miss Snake keeps an eye on the dancing. Everyone is eager to try out new jobs and can't wait for the evening to start. The ballet show is a big success and the audience are very impressed with the teamwork when they know a key member is missing. They give the friends an extra round of applause for doing such a good job. Clever Miss Snake!

Bats and Birds

During Summer the sun doesn't set until quite late in the evening. Jodie is wide-awake in bed even though it is ten o'clock and way past her bedtime. Jodie likes to listen to the birds twittering away before they settle down to sleep. This usually helps her to sleep too. But tonight the birds have quietened down and Jodie still doesn't feel tired.

She opens the curtains and looks out at the moon, in a sky that hasn't yet darkened completely.

She can just make out a few shadowy creatures flitting round and about the house. This puzzles Jodie because all the birds are asleep. What could they be? Mummy pops her head round the door and is surprised to find Jodie is still awake. Jodie says she can't sleep until the birds go to bed. Mummy looks out of the window and chuckles.

She picks a wildlife book from Jodie's bookcase and they read about bats.

When it's dark outside it is easy to mistake bats for birds. Bats are furry and they have leathery wings. They are almost blind but avoid bumping into things by making high-pitched squeaks. The noise bounces off objects and by listening to the echoes, bats can navigate safely. They are nocturnal and they like to hang upside down as they sleep. Jodie is also asleep now. She's upside down too with her feet on the pillow! Mummy tucks her up and kisses her goodnight.

Princess Poppy

Princess Poppy lives in a grand castle at the top of a steep hill. She is a very lucky little girl because she seems to have everything she could ever wish for. She has rooms full of toys and wardrobes filled with beautiful clothes and shoes. She has her very own hairdresser who accompanies her every minute of the day in case a hair strays out of place. She has dozens of personal servants and there is even someone to read her books to her!

Princess Poppy should be the happiest little girl in the world, but she is probably the most bored little girl in the world! Looking out of her bedroom window, high up in the tower, she sees the cook's three children helping with everyone's chores down in the yard. They look to be having so much fun. She decides to join them, so she picks out her prettiest dress and daintiest shoes and skips down the stairs to meet them. The children are helping the groom to clean the stables and they are covered in straw and dust.

When Poppy asks if she can join in they take one look at her pink dress, sparkly shoes and manicured nails and burst out laughing. Poppy turns to go before they see her tears. As she crosses the courtyard the groom feels sorry for her and hands her a pile of old clothes that he's grown out of. He tells her to come back when she's got changed. Poppy is back five minutes later and this time the children are happy to let her join in.

Poppy is grubby and tired after cleaning the stables and feeding the horses but she can't remember the last time she enjoyed herself so much. Now Poppy spends a lot of her time helping the groom, the gardener and the cook or just playing with her new friends. The children also like spending time in Poppy's room, with all her toys and books and they enjoy dressing up in Poppy's fabulous clothes. Poppy thinks it's much more fun to share and she loves being with her new friends.

Danny's Dinosaurs

Danny is dinosaur mad! He has a huge collection of plastic dinosaurs and he knows all their names, even the really long ones! Danny's teacher has asked all the children in his class to bring something in that interests them, so Danny brings in his dinosaur collection.

The teacher is very impressed with Danny's dinosaurs and asks him to tell his classmates a bit about them.

Danny tells everyone that the word dinosaur means 'thunder lizard'. These gigantic lizards lived 140 million years ago, before there were people on Earth! They came in all shapes and sizes, and they have wonderful names. He picks up the first dinosaur. 'This is a BRACHIOSAURUS, the biggest dinosaur ever. It was much, much taller than a house!'

TYRANNOSAURUS REX, was a very fierce dinosaur, which had teeth as long as a man's hand!

63

The PTERODACTYL was a flying dinosaur, with wings like a bat. Danny explains to the other children that the the 'p' in pterodactyl is silent. Next is TRICERATOPS, with its frilly neck made from bone, and its three horns. This is Danny's favourite. The COMPSOGNATHUS was the smallest dinosaur. It was about the size of a chicken. The last dinosaur is a PACHYCEPHALOSAURUS. Even Danny has trouble pronouncing that name! They are also called bone-heads because they used their heads as battering rams.

When Danny has finished, the teacher hands out paper and crayons and the children draw dinosaurs all morning. The teacher then unrolls a long piece of wallpaper and sticks the drawings all over it. Then the children colour in the background with trees and volcanoes and finally, they have a huge landscape, full of dinosaurs.

It looks fantastic and the children are so pleased. They all think dinosaurs are very interesting and they hope Danny will be able to bring his collection to school again soon!